YOU ONLY LIVE TWICE

"VOLUME III"

JASON TERHUNE

"EBONY"

Intro:

She is so damn beautiful, I can't help but just stare at her in the moon light. Just the mere sight of her almost makes me want to tremble. The greatest joy that I have ever known is that she is all mine, no other man can or will ever possess her. She is perfectly black, long dark and sexy. She has the most perfect curves that you have ever seen, anyone has ever seen, hand crafted by god himself. As I run my hand down her body my own body begins to shutter slightly. I hate saying this, and I have said that I never would say this, but I love her, yes, I am truly in love with her. I can't even begin to imagine what I would do, how I would feel if anything ever happened to her.

She smells so damn good, so fresh and so clean. I picked her up, I hold her, my sweet ebony princess is my 308 rifle. She is the perfect weight, and perfectly balanced. I put her butt to my shoulder, I peer through her scope, night vision capable of course. I am looking for a particular target, the target has to be perfect, and there can be no exception. If everything isn't perfect, the mission will be aborted.

My perfect Ebony princess is silenced, a joy that I only wish upon a woman. I love my silencer, yet it does have its drawbacks. When I silence my sweet Ebony it cuts back on her effective range. Not that this matters for me, I am surgical with my rifle at over a mile. I have Ebony doped in at around one thousand yards right now though, no need for a long range shot, no not here. My target is maybe seven or eight hundred yards away, right around a half a mile for all of you who can do simple math. Ebony was made to reach out and touch someone from a long distance, anything under a thousand yards is like shooting beer cans.

I will never forget when and where I first learned how to shoot. I was just a kid, it was the bridge just outside of town with all of the graffiti. I don't know if shooting beer cans floating down the creek made me a good shot, but it sure as hell taught me to hit a very small moving target. I assure you that a beer can floating with the current at over one hundred yards is a small target, especially with a 22. Looking back I guess that I did learn accuracy on that bridge. I know one thing shooting from that bridge definitely gave me a love for firearms. Shit, I haven't thought of that old bridge just outside of Wayne, Nebraska in years.

Wayne Nebraska, wow that seems like another life time ago. I am so, so different now, so very different. While once I stared into my scope it was out into an open corn field. Now, well now I am on the rooftop of the old Hunt Ridge building off of Charleston in Las Vegas, Nevada. To be honest, frank if you will, I prefer the open cornfields over this shit hole any day. There is nothing like a fall breeze and a big buck in your sights at five hundred yards. This place, well this place is just fucked.

As I look down on to the street with all of the shit that I see it takes every bit of me to not puke in my mouth. Near

every one that I see is a fucking junkie or
low life of some sort. Those who are not
actual junkies are the ones selling the
poison to the junkies. I taste the bile in
my mouth when I see some disgusting black
crack whore attempting to sell her pussy.
Some stupid suburban fuck in a mini-van is
attempting to work out an agreement for
what I am sure is aids infested pussy. You
can always tell the people who don't belong
here, they only show up at night. Honkies
from the burbs trying to buy drugs, pussy,
god only knows what else.

     Nothing is done about this foul shit,
the fucking pigs don't give two fucks.
Those pieces of shit will send out the swat

team to bust some fool for weed, yet turn
their eyes to the dregs of society and the
cancers that comes with them right before
their eyes. Well tonight that is all about
to change, everything is about to change.
Tonight I declare war on these fucking
pigs, on the government, I declare war on
society itself. I already know in the end I
will lose this war. Yet I will inspire
thousands, this is far bigger than myself.
When I die, and I will die, it will be one
life for the cause, one life, my life is
worth losing for the freedom of all my
people.

Finally, exactly what I have been
waiting for. Looking through my scope I can

see a fucking pig talking to a dealer through his window. I can see sergeant stripes on his uniform, a fucking Sergeant laughing it up with a dope dealer.

This bastard isn't busting this piece of shit, no he is here for his nightly kickback. I can see each and every one of their facial expressions through my scope. He is a white boy, even through the night vision I can tell he has light eyes and what looks like light brown hair. I can see him laughing it up with the dealer, their normal routine. Oh Ebony I love you my sweet, make daddy proud. As the fucking pig is leaning back laughing I pull the trigger. My bullet is true, his fucking head explodes all over the inside of the squad car, covering the dealer in brain matter as well. Good riddance you fucking piece of shit, I laugh. It seems that on this street it is only I who has taken an oath to protect and serve the people tonight.

No time to enjoy my work, I quickly break Ebony down into her seven beautiful pieces. I make my way down the stairs and throw the bag with Ebony in it into my shopping cart filled with all of the smelly ass random shit any bum would have. I am dressed the part, down to the filth on my skin and clothes. I make my way down the alley as any bum would. No one notices the homeless, no they are all invisible thus I am invisible. Shit, even if a cop did stop me right now with all of the foul smelling shit in my cart no cop would dare touch me or my things. Shit, even I am disgusted by how bad I smell right now.

Chap. 1

Sitting on the rooftop of my apartment complex I am watching the sunrise. So few people have ever really watched the sun rise. Hell, there was a time in my life when even I hadn't really actually watched the glory of the new day. That was then though, before I had my great awakening if you will. Like so many people I was blinded to all of the bullshit that I had been force fed since the day that I was born. I like so many bought into the system, I was just as ignorant as everyone else. Purchase this, fear this, don't step out of line always do as you are told. Never worry about the real world, it's scary out there but your government will always protect you. Don't be scared Citizen X, stay inside your house and watch your big screen, The Voice is on. Do not forget to go to Walmart Citizen, do your duty, consume and obey.

Do not worry if you don't have the money, buy everything on credit, you can afford it. Do not worry about church, we the government will tell you all you need to know about god. All you need do is watch Ancient Aliens good citizen. What a fucking joke, everything is just a big scam.

I'm not quite sure when it was that I woke up from this fucked off dream we call life. I do know it was as if I had been hit by a speeding truck. Upon impact everything came clear to me, my eyes were opened. I knew at that moment for the first time in my life that I was actually awake. To be honest the whole experience was rather scary, imagine seeing everything all at once. I likened my awakening to me being a puppy pulled from its mother's tit. The entire world changed before my eyes, I saw

past the lies that the newscaster reported,
past the all of the lies we were all being
told. I actually saw the chemical filled
air, took in a deep breath of the
pollution. I longed for fresh air but knew
I still had to breathe. I saw the
government for what it was, a police state.

The worse aspect of all of this was
that I saw my fellow man for the first time
in my life. I saw how far we had all
fallen, how pathetic we had become as a
species. I now knew that we were all
connected, yet this was kept from us. The
powers that be feared our spiritual
evolution. I tried not to look upon
everyone with contempt, they were just

sleeping still. I was like them at one point, now I am awake, I had evolved. I felt a true connection to everyone and everything, I was one with the universe. I tried to look on my fellow man as equals but I knew the truth. The truth is that I am evolved, I am the next level of evolution, they are all simple Neanderthals.

By the time that I got home from my declaration of war, my single act of justice was all over the news. Never in Vegas hell probably America had a cop been the victim of a sniper attack. The city is in an uproar, yet quietly many cheer my action. I don't cheer death, in fact I hate death, I hate violence in general, yet I know they both have their time and place. In the end I feel no more pity for the ape that I killed than a child does stepping on an ant. Close ancestor or not does the company scientist feel pity for the chimp they put toxic make up on to make sure it won't eat holes into a rich bitches face? All that matters is this moment, all that matters is the blues turning to purples. Purples turning to pinks, then to different hues of oranges. Finally everything turning yellows to blue, the beautiful bright blue that is the Vegas sky. The beautiful blue sky that tops the mountains that embrace our sweet valley like big arms giving us a

hug. I so love the sunrise, the glory of
yet another new day being born from the
darkness.

Chap. 2

Part two of my plan will soon come to
pass. The system that I have declared war
on truly only cares about one thing and one
thing only, money. Money equals power,
power is an end to a means. As of late I
have seen the powers that be begin to buy
up all of the food and fresh water
supplies. Then they turn around and jack
the prices way up. The public takes little
to no notice of all of this. I am not

surprised, people seldom look past the contents of their wallets. I can't let this slip, even it has slipped past the masses.

I have already used my bum disguise, it is time for something new. No this time I will use my little old man costume. Like a bum no one really ever wants to look at the elderly. The elderly are a walking reminder that we are all going to one day die. When a feeble old man walks up to you it is a look into your own future. No one wants to see that their future is bleak, no one wants to see the ravages of age. No, we all want to think that we will be forever young, forever beautiful.

I leave my apartment and head downtown. For those of you who are not from Vegas downtown is not the strip, yet it is a part of the same evil beast. I pack up all of my essentials inside of my backpack and hop into my car. From my place downtown is pretty quick to get to, maybe ten minutes to the 95 freeway, from there maybe a fifteen minuet drive north. I love getting on the freeway in my big old boat of a car. Hell, I even enjoy all of the traffic as odd as that sounds. I have always seen freeways as a cities arteries, downtown being its heart. I have always wondered though just where the hell all these people have to go on the freeway with me. The funny thing isn't that they all have to go at the same time as you.

I cruise along the freeway pretty well unimpeded by the traffic till I near the spaghetti bowl. It's no real worry though the Las Vegas Downtown exit is right before the thick of it all. As I pull off of the freeway I see a Vegas of long ago, even a sign that simply reads Elvis slept here. These old casinos once ruled this land, now they are like relics. To look at these relics now compared to those on the strip one would play hell to see this once held glory. I remember Grandma telling me how her and her friends all sat atop the Vegas Club and watched bombs going off. Damn, that was so long ago, yet to her it is just a blink of an eye.

I pull into the all day long free parking lot just north of Fremont Street on Main Street. One of the few things that people know is that underneath all of downtown as well as the strip is a vast network of tunnels. Some of these are used for drainage, some for wiring, some for passage, others, well who knows what for. Just past the railroad tracks by what is obviously a FIMA camp is an entrance to these tunnels. I quickly drop down into the tunnels making sure that no one see's me.

        After climbing down what I estimate to
be a story I am on the main floor. I turn
on my flash light and begin to inspect my
surroundings. My hiding spot is an old
abandoned electrical room from years gone
past just off of the main shaft. Once
inside I take out my mirror and begin to
apply all of my makeup. I begin by lighting
my skin tone and adding random liver spots.
I make sure to do my hands as well, few
people ever do their hands. Along with this
I put wrings under my eyes as well as build
shadow lines to give the illusion of
wrinkles. There it is I tell myself, time
for my green slacks, tan off brown flannel
shirt, and of course white Velcro shoes. I

then place a white beard on my face with some decent movie prop glue, along with a fucked off wig under my NRA hat. Last but not least I place a pair of those oversized old people sunglasses on, or more real in my opinion visors. The transformation is complete, I for all points and purposes appear to be a seventy year old plus man. To top off the uniform I even have your stereo typical Fresh and Easy reusable bag with on my side as I make my way back onto the city streets. No one would ever suspect that inside of this bag is a loaded and silenced MP5 along with ten extra clips. This coupled with the two nine millimeters

hidden under my shirt and five clips apiece
extra makes me armed and fucking dangerous.

I make my way down Bridger Street at a
slow pace. That is the hardest part,
walking like I am old. My target is the
Wells Fargo on Bridger and Las Vegas BLVD.
I have chosen this bank due to their own
arrogance. Most of the other banks in town
have moved to bullet proof glass enclosing
the workers from the guest, this bank with
its zero fear of being robbed has chosen
not to follow suit. I guess they figure
first that they are on Las Vegas BLVD, then
they are only two blocks from the cop shop.
These facts coupled with the obvious fact
they are a stone's throw from the Federal

building. To be real with you who would be stupid enough to hit this place? Shit, as I see it all these aspects that would scare off anyone else only make my job easier.

As I walk into the bank I am greeted by a large security guard. He is a black man, probably in his mid to late forties, he seems like a nice guy really. Once inside of the bank I bend down, no one takes notice of me as I pull out my MP5. I open up with a three round burst into the chest of the nice security guard. I then turn on the customers and shoot three of them down as if they were nothing but lowly dogs. I rush the counter and leap over, I have been in the bank now less than fifte seconds. I look, no blinking lights, no alarms have been pressed yet. I order the girl to fill my bag with only loose bills and fill it fast. I don't want to risk a dye pack or any sort of tracking device, thus why I ordered loose bills only. One teller tries to run, no mercy is shown, I open up with a three round burst into the back of her head. Her head pops like a watermelon, her brains spraying all over the room. My bag is full of cash, I look at the three remaining tellers and thank them for their service. I then open fire into each one of them, their bodies hit the floor like bags of flour. One girl is trying to crawl away after being shot. I admire her strength as well as her courage. This doesn't detour me from placing the barrel of my gun to her head and letting a bullet enter her brain. I quickly take my gun and throw it into its bag and walk out the door. The inside of the bank is now a fucking blood bath, I leave no one alive to tell my tail other than the video camera.

I quickly make my way back to the tunnels, I know it is a matter of moments before someone stumbles onto my work. Once again I am in darkness, the safety of the Las Vegas underground. I was inside of the bank a total of ninety one seconds, one second too long. They say a bank job should never take over ninety seconds, well the movies and the internet anyway. I quickly strip off all of my clothes, and wipe myself clean of any and all makeup. I wore gloves the whole time so I left no finger prints. I am inside of my secret chamber, I am safe here.

I have no clue as to just how long it will take the pigs to get to the bank? All I know is that I am already making my way through the tunnels away from downtown towards the strip. My car will be fine among the thousands of others cars for the time being. Right now I have everything inside of my back pack, with my Ohio State hoodie I look like any and every tourist in town right now. I don't even spend twenty minutes in the tunnels and I am by the Wynn blending in with all of the other tourist, fuck I am even taking photos, mission accomplished. It may seem fucked up what I just did, but I don't care one bit. I am justified in my heart and soul for my actions, thus they do not matter, despite the severity. You see I am at war, thus I am in a constant state of war, mind, body, and soul. The bank, well the bank is part of the enemy force, all those inside were enemy combatants. I am a soldier, I am a warrior, and those who die by my hands do so in combat, ensuring them a glorious death. The reality is that there are no innocents in this war, not even myself.

Two hundred and forty seven thousand three hundred and eighty six dollars. This is the take that I got from my Wells Fargo robbery. The city is now in an even bigger uproar than with the cop after seeing the surveillance video, shit it had even been linked on to you tube. The Feds as well as local pigs are all freaking out, first that there is no DNA, then that there are no prints. As if I wouldn't have been smart enough to wash my body with bleach and wear gloves, I watch CIS. If they did get any sort of print they would be the fake

partials I placed on the gloves myself. All
I saw on the news was how brutal the
robbery was, I even made the national news,
and so did the cop killing. The cop killing
got me fans, the bank got me some as well,
most of all it was fear that was instilled
in the masses. Money, the news said I did
it all for money, fuck, money is just
worthless paper to me. I hate money,
although this money is already earmarked
for a greater purpose. I did not kill those
people for money though, no I did it to
make a point, had they lived no true fear
would have been instilled, thus I would
have failed my mission.

Over the years I have made friends with, even gotten in good with a group of Somali cab drivers here in the city. While I never once believed in their rhetoric or their religious bullshit I under stood their frustrations. Like me they too believe that they are at war, unlike me they are far too much of a pack of pussies to do anything other than talk about it. These fucking idiots have every weapon known to god, shit that even scared the fuck out of me, yet despite having all of this cool ass shit they are afraid to use it. Over the last few years I have been purchasing groups of random weapons from them, at great rock bottom prices to. Now with the bank job I have all the cash and then some to get everything that I ever needed. I know that I can't leave any of these fools alive after though, they will crack under pressure, rag head jihadi rhetoric or not. For a second I find myself in a bit of a moral pickle, I actually like a few of these guys, but hey this is war.

I called up Samir from one of my many prepay phones I get from the Walmart off of Marks and Sunset. Remember that despite your phone being prepay they can still track it, prepay just makes it a little bit harder. In the end they will get you with voice recognition, but that is only if they really want you. As long as you always call from public spots your cool, the GPS will read Walmart or the mall, common ground. I tell Samir to meet me with his Koran for a study session, he knows exactly what I mean. We have already worked out a price for the Koran on a previous meeting, I am cool. I like Samir but of course I don't trust him, I trust no one. I can't trust anyone at all, hell not even myself. The one thing that I do trust is Samir's greed. While he claims to be some holy jihad warrior, I know that money is his only true god. This being the case I tell him to meet me at his normal spot out at Lake Mead. Lake Mead is the perfect spot to meet Samir. I have my boat docked out there, well of course it isn't actually my boat per say. Not only is it not my boat if you will, no one that I know has any clue that it even exist. This boat has proven to be the perfect place to stash all of the goods I have procured from Samir. People can't look for shit if they have no clue as to where it may be.

When Samir shows up we are alone at the camp ground. I have already scouted everything out. This all used to be under water just a few years ago. It is crazy the drought had moved the shore near a thousand yards from its previous boundary. I am excited when Samir shows me all that he has brought for me. First, sixty pounds of C4

with timed blasting caps. Second, two
actual one hundred pound containers of
nerve gas, the same shit used on the Kurds
he insisted. Third, five AR 15's, five
pistols, ten silencers, and lastly some Del
Taco I had asked him to grab.

I am not sure how to use the Nerve Gas
but Samir shows me how to use the timers.
He laughs telling me it is as easy as using
a kitchen timer, he is actually right it is
just like a kitchen timer. I guess one must
always remember that soldiers are regular
people, things must always be dumbed down.
I mean fuck, they are products of the
American Miss-education system.

I am wearing fake prints over my fingertips, making sure that I touch the money as much as possible. My whole hand is covered in an almost invisible latex so as not to leave any DNA traces. You see the prints that I am wearing today were downloaded and printed on the latex via my printer. I was sure to download the prints of a pretty high up officer within the Metro Police department. I wanted this money to get circulated, yet not too much, just enough to get back to the Feds. Samir ask where I have gotten all of the cash, I just smiled and say that I won it at the Casino. He knows it is best not to really know the truth. Despite this his mere asking makes me question shooting him right then and there. I can see the greed in his eyes as he looks upon the cash, just under one hundred thousand dollars. One hundred thousand dollars, the cut rate for a van load of goodies from a want a bee Somali terrorist, pretty damn good deal if you ask me.

Samir and I quickly part ways as soon as our business is finished. Both of us know it is best not to get picked up with any of what we have, either one of us. After stashing all of my new toys on my boat I quickly make my way back into the city. It is soon going to be time to initiate phase two of my plans involving my dear friend Samir.

I know that Samir is a fucking idiot and will start blowing cash like a fool as soon as he can. While I want this to get those prints out there I don't want it to come back to him too quickly. My end goal is to get the prints out there but not get Samir caught at all. I know that fool will drop a dime in an instant. I can't allow Samir to get caught by the cops or the Feds, if he did I couldn't get to him before he rolled over on me. Knowing he would be facing a life term I was sure he would, the idea is to let him blow some quickly then take his stupid ass out.

It is just after midnight, I load up my bag, hop on my Kawasaki Ninja 1000 and head off into the night. Samir isn't really all that far from me, he lives in a shit hole little house over on the East Side. I always liked that side of town to be honest, be it poor Mexican or not. What is good for me is that these people rarely ever call the police, no matter what they hear or saw they know to keep their mouths shut.

I pull into the alley and hide my bike. Dressed in all black I quickly make my way over Samir's wall unseen. I put my night vision glasses on as I use the shadows as camouflage. Darkness conceals

all the beast of the night, I am here to do
evil thus I am a beast. In total darkness I
pull back the lever on my MP5, and chamber
a round. Darkness and silence, my two best
friends, my MP5, dark like Ebony, beautiful
like Ebony, my wife. I make my way into an
open window, I see two men sleeping on the
floor that I have never seen before. I am a
thief in the night, here to steal their
very lives.

Without any hesitation I place the
barrel of my gun against the head of the
first man on the floor and pull the
trigger. I am sprayed with brain matter and
blood covering my dark leather outfit. In
an instant I drop three silenced rounds

into the chest of the second man sleeping. He never even got the chance to wake up, for the best really. I see a knife on the floor, it hits me, I stab it into the light socket killing all power in the house.

I open the door and make my way into the hall. I see only two shut doors. I open the first door, there are two more men sleeping on makeshift beds on the floor. My noise hasn't woken them up, I am lucky. I have no time to waste I quickly put a three round burst into each one of their heads. The second man had looked up startled, he received his round in the face. I had hope they would both know the joy of simply waking up dead, a joy I am sure that

neither one of them deserved.

I make my way back into the hall,

working my way silently to the last

bedroom. I get up to the door and am privy

to a joyous sound. From the door I can hear

a voice I know to be Samir's, along with

that of a woman, ah my little rag head

buddy is getting some pussy, I laugh to

myself. Slowly I turn the knob to the door

then fling it open. I let go pulling the

trigger on entry filling Samir with six

bullets, killing him instantly. Lucky

fucker he got to go with a hard dick that

is a nice way to go.

The whore is some white crack head looking bitch. I am surprised Samir didn't spring for something better with all of the money I gave him. She is on her knees, begging me to spare her life, so much so that it is pathetic. I tell her to look forward, then I ask her, what have you done in your life that makes it worth saving my sweet? With that I pulled the trigger blowing her brains out of the place where her face used to be. I did a good thing killing her, I freed her from a horrible existence. I probably saved some dudes life from the aids I am sure she had.

I then make a quick check of the house, there is no one left alive. I almost shit myself when I see that all of the money except around ten grand is all laid out on the kitchen table. I take half of the money and make my way out the door. Perfect, these fucking Somali's were about to take at least a partial rap on the bank job. All I know is that the shit is about to hit the fan soon. Once the pigs find that place with all of the cash and weapons as well as all of their jihad shit, well fuck. That shit will go down as a terrorist cell taken down in Vegas, at least that is what the news will say.

Just before I hit the freeway I make a call on one of my prepay cell phones. I call the pigs and tell them that I heard gun shots coming from Samir's address. Doing eighty down the freeway I threw the phone over my shoulder letting it smash to pieces on the concrete. When I get home I pull into my garage and put my plate back on my bike. I go inside, I am tired, this shit takes a lot out of you. All in all everything went perfect tonight. I can't wait to see the morning news.

Chap. 4

The next morning I wake up and go straight to the TV. The local and national news is fucking overwhelming, the shit is on every channel. I am amazed that my nights little adventure is on both Fox and

CNN. All of the channels are talking about

a terrorist cell in Las Vegas Nevada. Of

course they are saying that they are the

ones who had taken out Samir and his

buddies. The money has already been traced

to the robbery, shit as going my way. Vegas

is a gambling town, now and again you just

have to roll the dice. This time it looks

as if the dice just rolled my way. I had no

clue but those Somali fucks had a decent

cash of chemical weapons. This coupled with

all of the other jihadist shit and the

press was having a field day. I have to

laugh, it seems that maybe Samir and his

buddies were semi-serious. Who would have

guessed it? To be honest, I thought they were all talk.

This is great for me, I can now keep on doing my missions. The Feds and the pigs are chasing their own tails now, the press is right on their heels. Everyone is on edge watching for rag heads. Samir's neighbor was on TV talking about how he had never trusted them at all. He is going on about how they were all weird and kept to themselves, making them seem that more evil.

I almost feel bad for Samir, I almost felt bad about killing him, but it was for the best. The news says how they thought that the robbery money was used to purchase weapons. I am off the hook for a while, at least in the eyes of the pigs and the news. I know that they are really looking for me. They just aren't putting the truth out for the public, I can't blame them really.

I have two missions left before I will be going into hiding for a while. I figure if I want this to last I will have to take out a page in the book of the Unabomber. You see he only lasted because he went into hiding, self-reclusion. He would go out, commit his acts of terror, then he disappeared into the woods for years. That will be me, I know that one day I will get caught, I know that I will be killed, I just want to prolong that day from happening, at least for a while. The key to years of success is to be a ghost. Randomly I will haunt the land, but most of the time I will simply be a thought in the back of your mind.

I spent near ten years walking nearly all of the underground tunnels here in Vegas. I made physical maps at first, then with years of exploring I made mental maps. This didn't always work though, I remember a few of my first times with no maps, shit I got lost once for two days. It seems fitting to be down in the tunnels. The moist air, the darkness, the rats and of course the bugs, reminds me of my childhood. Down in the tunnels I feel as if I am already dead, simply walking the halls of my tomb.

Often I always think about how nice it would have been if I were never woken up. I could be just like everyone else. I could sit around, drink beer, watch football, the normal guy shit. That is only a dream now, the moment that I saw the light I was fucked. I always knew that there would never be any turning back, no going back to my old life. It is better this way honestly. I am proof that free will does not exist. No, everything has been planned out by some higher power, some god if you will. I like you are just a pawn in a giant game of chess, ever moving closer to that final check mate.

My bag is so heavy right now, it is eighty pounds, yet it feels like five hundred. I remember when I was back in boot camp, we would carry half of our weight on our backs, not to mention the rest of our gear. Look at me now, here whining carrying less than one hundred pounds. It seems even heavier being hunched over in these damn tunnels.

It takes me nearly an hour to get where I need to go. I need to be at point one building one thirty nine, F as in Federal. You would think that these fools

would actually make it a lot harder to get
into a Federal buildings lower levels. I am
so tired that I simply sit my ass down for
a little while and catch my breath. I am
happy though, all of this hard work is
actually over. I have been working on this
for years. During this time I have placed
ten fifty gallon drums of anhydrous
fertilizer coupled up to each support beam.
I have also mixed the fertilizer with sixty
pounds of C4. The two of these coupled
together, well let's just say that this
building will drop faster than a dress on
prom night. All and all it is a simple plan
really, any fool could do it really. You
see everyone always gives those damn rag

heads far too much credit. All I did was be a bit sneaky, find a weakness, and then work to exploit it. This is how terrorism works, believe me if I can do it anyone can do it.

The Federal buildings supports are all exposed at the basement level just above the tunnel. No one ever has gone this deep underground, not even the maintenance people. They would never have any reason to come down here, no one would. On each of the four main center beams I have placed ten pounds of C4 along with a fifty gallon drum of my anhydrous. I figure due to my calculations this shit should blow sky high. After I did this I placed my other two barrels along with the rest of my C4 directly in the middle of the room.

I enjoy making bombs, it is a very Zen process, as crazy as that sounds. How bomb making is Zen is that each and every step must be perfectly thought out. To make a bomb you must have a complete sense of complete mindfulness. I sit and work with each of my babies for close to an hour. It is hot down here in the belly of the beast, real hot. Yet I try not to let it bother me. I have no time to worry about trivial items such as heat. I am one hundred percent involved with my bomb making, by the time I finish my last bomb it is already nine thirty at night.

This is perfect for me, plenty of time to get home. In exactly twelve hours my little babies will blow, just in time for all of the employees to make it to their offices. Oh that Monday morning struggle, everyone in their offices slaving away. Little do they know soon they will all blown to fucking pieces. I have planned this out for the last two years, to be honest I am extremely excited to see my plan finally come to be. Happy that my babies are all ready to go I set their timers to go off at ten AM. I sit down in the center of the room on my knees and looked up to the heavens.

"Lord, I am doing your bidding, for it was only you who could have awoken me. Please lord grant me many bodies, allow me to fill your halls with souls."

With that prayer I get up and make my way through the tunnels. Before leaving the room I douse everything with ammonia to get rid of any DNA it always amazes me how much DNA that people leave behind at the scene of a crime. Fucking idiots, we all have cable, we all watch the same shows, take notes you fucking idiots.

The next day I awake with the vigor of a schoolboy. To be real I am surprised that I was able to sleep at all. I feel like a child waiting for Santa. I have been planning this now for over two years, working tirelessly to attain my goal. Today my mission will be realized, today I will know the joy of a goal achieved. I know that no matter what I do my morning will not go any faster. I decide to go about my normal morning routines. I put my gym clothes on and head out to hit LVAC. I love Monday, that is chest and shoulders day.

Once at the gym I hit my chest and shoulders out as hard as I possibly can. I know that my work out is suffering a bit due to my lack of concentration, but that is life. I try to lose myself in my IPOD bumping my favorite Hank III album. I love working out, yet I wish that I did it just for fun, no, even my work out has an end to a means. I know that I one day will have to be out in the wilderness, I will need my strength. That or if I end up in prison I will need my strength to fight to keep my asshole cherry. While either one of these circumstances are not ideal, they are both realities that I do face.

Weights are done to build strength, running on the treadmill near ten miles a day is to build endurance. Along with this I take jujitsu as well as krav Maga, and of course hot yoga for that bit of Zen in my life. I eat only organic when possible, no sugars. I try and eat only the meat that I personally hunt and kill. I am the perfect man. As far as I am concerned I am living as man is supposed to.

After the gym I make my way home and hop in the shower. Going to the gym was smart, people saw me out and about, I had an alibi. I love a hot shower, wash off the previous days transgressions. Shit, shower, and shave the three activities each man must do daily. Normally I love the three task, yet today all I can think about is my baby girls. Soon they will all detonate, taking down the local Federal building. I can't wait, my only fear is that I will not be able to hear the explosions from my apartment so far away from downtown.

Finally, it is nine fifty nine PM I walk out onto my porch and look off towards downtown. I close my eyes and take in a deep breath. I block out all of the noises from the street, there is nothing only silence. There are no more cars, no more birds, and no more workmen over across the street at the golf course, only sweet silence. The silence reminds me of Nebraska at night, I miss this silence, hell I miss Nebraska.

I take in a deep breath, I hear the explosion, more like a deep echo off in the distance. I look out over the golf course, I can see the smoke rising, I am filled with joy. I quickly turn on the TV and wait for the news. I then walk outside with all of my neighbors and act like I have no clue what is going on. Once again I have an alibi this way.

It don't take long and the news is already showing the bombing. They aren't saying it is a bombing just yet, but they know it is. The place is in shambles, over half of the building has collapsed the rest is on fire. The whole area is utter chaos that is the only way to explain the scene. As I watch on the TV I see bodies burning, parts of what used to be living people are strewn all around. It is a scene of utter beauty. I have no clue just yet how many people have lost their lives. If I get my wish not one person will have survived, but there are always a few.

I watched the TV all day long. I am glued to the news. With each passing hour it is evident that it was an act of terrorism. The TV is already saying it was possibly an act of the Somali terror cell, a few who escaped the courageous police. Ha, well, let them talk I laugh. Finally the tallies are in, over one thousand people dead at current count, the body count is expected to climb. There are three hundred people injured most in critical condition. I am excited about the body count, I had hoped for no survivors, but one thousand dead bodies, that's not bad if you ask me.

I want to take credit for what I have done, but that would be utter suicide. Two groups have already tried to take credit for my work, fucking wonderful dicks. These fucking so called terrorist trying to take credit for others work. Oh well, I guess that they won't look my way, I guess that is a good thing. Better to have every pig in the nation looking for Somali terrorist than my white ass.

This is cause for celebration, my mission has been accomplished. Everything has gone off without a hitch, god has allowed me to do his work. I decide to go and get some sushi, there is this awesome little all you can eat sushi spot by my house. As I knock down my first few sushi rolls I am happy. I close my eyes and thank

god for all of the glorious gifts that he
has bestowed upon me.

Chap. 6

Over the next few weeks I find it
smart to lay low. I have one more mission
to accomplish then it will be time to dip
out for a while. I have little real choice
anyway. Everything has worked out
perfectly, the lease on my apartment is up
in less than a month anyway. I figure it is
perfect, put all my shit in storage, pay
for a year and dip out for six months or

so, hell maybe for good. My plan is pretty sound as far as I am concerned.

Three days before my next mission I will board a plane for San Francisco. Once there I will get my hotel room. I will be sure to talk and to the employees and tip well. I will have an alibi, I was vacationing in Frisco. While my room is there I will board a Grey Hound back to Vegas, under a fake name of course. Once here I will carry out my next mission. I will retrieve a car that I have stashed in one of my storage units, a beautiful 2004 Corvette. I will throw my bags in my car and head out onto to the open road towards

Nebraska. I have been wanting to go home for a while anyway.

My next mission is one that will surely ensure me first rate passage into hell. People are accustomed to seeing people shot, even blown up, as fucked up as that is. While a lot of people originally tripped out about the pig I sniped, well that was just a ripple in a small pond really. The bombing, well hey I loved it and it was a great success, but people are used to that, no real fear involved. Shit they are still showing that shit nightly on all of the news channels, score for me. I guess maybe people are scared that someone bombed the Vegas Federal building. That was never the end goal though, no my end goal was to get people to be afraid to come here, to affect their money. Money is all that matters to the powers that be. The Feds are tripping, no one has enacted any acts of terror against the government in decades.

I have declared war, and my declaration has defiantly been heard. Now what I am about to do is beyond fucked up. Far worse than anything I have done as of yet. Samir had sold me two very large containers of weapons grade toxic nerve gas, it is time to put them to use. The best thing is that four other cans had been found at Samir's place, once again they will be looking for Somali's.

My plan is simple really, at least in theory, my plan is to release the toxic nerve gas into the Las Vegas Metropolitan Police Station. If all goes well everyone in the building will die a very horrible death. I know that this will not go unnoticed. Hell, the shit I got from Samir is more toxic than that shit used in Syria just recently. With this one act I will bring down the entire weight of the United States Government upon me, or Samir's people anyway. To be honest I am pretty sure that the entire world will be down on me for this one. A small price to pay for

doing the work of god, a small price to pay
for waking thousands of people up. Just
seeing someone fight back, knowing that
they too can, well that is why I am doing
this.

After I get all of my shit into
storage I make my way to and back from
Frisco as fast as possible. I know that I
won't be able to use the tunnels again, no
the pigs have closed those down now. I
decide that my B plan will be best for me,
more dangerous, but attainable.

For a while I have been driving around
in a fake contractor's truck, set up as an
electrical service. I have even been in and

out of the Cop shop multiple times acting as if I have been working. People have seen me there before, thus I am invisible. There is no time like the present, I put my disguise on, the uniform, the dark makeup, a fake wig under my hat, I now work for Mojave Electrical. I look like a Mexican, dark skin, dark contacts, dark wig, I am not myself any longer. When you make yourself look dark people only see dark skin, a Mexican, well they look like seventy five percent of the world. Not being racist, just using peoples random racism to my own advantage.

I make my way to the Metro Police station down on Martin Luther King. I push my cart in and no one even looks twice at me or even attempts to stop me. It's rare that people stop a man who looks like he is doing his job. I even stop to take a piss, of course I don't touch my dick at all, I am wearing my latex gloves, the invisible kind. As always I have downloaded finger prints and printed them onto my gloves.

In maybe ten minutes I am on the roof and opening up the air conditioning unit. This is so damn easy that anyone with little to no planning could have done this. Poor arrogant fools. I am in the middle of the hornet's nest, the one place where they have no fear. It's funny, hornet's nest or not they still need security.

Once I have the air conditioning units open I connect my hoses to the nerve gas. My two hundred pounds of compressed toxic nerve gas will soon be spread throughout the entire building, fucked up I know. I set the timer for thirty minutes. That leaves me exactly enough time to get back to my truck and on the freeway.

I almost feel bad as I ride the elevator down to the main lobby. As I walk out the door and load up my truck I take one last look at my watch. I have fifteen minutes left, plenty of time. I quickly hop on the freeway and begin to head north to my storage unit. Once at my unit I pull in and lock up the unit. I go to my next unit and pull out my corvette. Inside of the truck there is a bomb set for twenty four hours from now. I have already washed the truck down with ammonia to clear any DNA. I have made fifty gallons of napalm, there will be nothing left of this whole unit, hell the entire building, let alone the truck.

This storage spot is one of those that ask no questions, no names, no cameras, just pay in cash. I hop in my Corvette and head North on the fifteen freeway. The radio is already reporting some sort of a chemical attack at the Metro Police Station. All of Martin Luther King has been shut down, no one can go in or go out.

I have set the cans to blow one hour after they let loose their payload. Now the radio is talking about an explosion atop the Police Station. I have left nothing to chance. Descriptions of the police officers foaming at the mouth, skin all green, lips curled up, dying in agony fills the airwaves. There is even talk that some of their eyeballs had popped clear out of their heads, clear out of their fucking heads can you believe that? The number of dead has not been released two hours later as I pull into St. George. There are no suspects as of yet according to the police, not that they would release it anyway yet.

Once again Somali terrorist are being suspected, fools.

As I drive into Colorado I do so with a smile. I had purchased dope and then had it sold for me with my money from the robbery. Right now I am sitting on over two hundred grand of clean money in my car. I feel good, I am heading back to Nebraska. I haven't had a vacation in years, I am due for one. My last mission had gone perfect, I look forward to hearing about how many people I killed, not that I really care. I will come home to Vegas in three or four months most likely, it's hard for me to stay away from the V Town. That and the moment it gets cold I am certain to turn tail and run back to the desert. Until then though I will be drinking Natural Ice beer and fishing with some good old friends. It's time to be a ghost.

"Buzz of the Street Light"

Intro:

I sit alone in the dimly lit room. The room is dark, not to dark, but dark enough. No, once you allow your eyes to adjust you can see the outline of the room, a few items here and there. There is a bed, nothing fancy at all, just something to lay on at best. Personally I would say that the bed is just slightly more comfortable than the floor. Often like far too many of the women I have sex with, only slightly better than masturbation. A fan in the corner of the room blows the stale semi rank smelling air throughout the room from side to side, making a clacking sound as it does so. The room wreaks of old farts and dirty clothes. The fan only heightens this fact. Despite this I still find myself far too lazy to actually get up and turn the fan off. I want to turn on the TV but am reluctant to do so. It seems rare that anything good is ever actually on TV. I am sure that if I actually get the nerve up to turn it on, that it will only disappoint me at best. Most likely I will hear about what new war we are getting into. That or I will hear about how some fucking lunatic ran into a school or mall again and started blowing people away. Either way I find it far easier just to leave the TV off, a decision I have rarely regretted in life.

As I see it the world is or possibly already has gone to shit. The only hard part is actually attempting to figure out exactly when it all had happened. The actual point in time is what I can't put my finger on, just when did everything go to shit? Most people like to blame Bush, but

it all started long before his dumb ass.
No, I heard all of the hippie whining
bullshit about how it was Bush who drug us
into multiple wars. All these hippies are
always saying it is Bush's fault so many
have died or been wounded, blah, blah,
blah. Personally as far as I see it those
who got killed got lucky. How many people
came back without legs and arms and shit?
Even worse how many people came back fucked
in the head, the wounds that you can't see
rarely heal.

The guys from Nam all came back
fucked, not like these new guys though. No
I may sound like a dick but the men during
the Nam era were stronger, far worse ass

than people these days. Even I am a victim,
my generation was the first to be purposely
made into pussies. The sad reality now is
that you need not go to war to see blood in
the streets. America, hell the world has
changed, violence, people going crazy, just
fucked up shit in general is now the norm.

None of this matters though, no none
of this matters at all to be real with you.
The truth is it's all by design, making us
into fat, lazy, docile, pussies that is. As
I see it, at this moment there are no other
moments. The only moment, the only true
moment is the one at this precise second.
If any of this even exist at all? One must
always remember that there is no past,

there is no future, and if there is a future it isn't promised to you anyway. No, all that exist is this very moment, this precise point in your existence.

At this moment all that matters to me is the hum of the street light outside of my window, mixed with the sound of random traffic interwoven within it. In an odd way it is beautiful to look at. The idea that something so taken for granted can be so beautiful glowing all white with its semi ere sheen around it. I know it sounds stupid, but I assure you that it means everything to me right now. I am taken into my own past which may or may not exist, am I still grounded in this moment? I am a young man, no I am a boy back in Wayne

Nebraska. I am in my dingy basement hovel

which was supposed to be a bedroom. The

reality is that it is a disgusting shit

hole covered in filth, a cracked foundation

wall allows the cold air to flow in, my

friends are rats and mice, along with

millions of cockroaches. I am on the water

bed I got from my aunt Kathy, "rest her

soul", looking out my small broken prison

like window. I see the street light in

front of my house, glowing all beautiful, a

thing of beauty in my young heart and soul.

The light glows not bright but radiant if

that makes sense? Maybe it is just the way

the light cuts through the Nebraska

humidity with its countless swarms of bugs circling her, or maybe it is just the imagination of a young boy.

It was seeing that light from my small prison like window in my shitty basement hovel in Wayne Nebraska that allowed me to be free. Within that light I would lose myself in meditation, long before I even knew what meditation even was. Looking at the glow of the light I didn't notice the filthy hoarders nest in which I was forced to live. I didn't notice the rats, I didn't notice the mice, and I didn't even notice the dam roaches. I didn't notice the mounds of clothes decomposing into the floor, returning to a state of dirt or what I saw

as stinky sludge. I didn't notice the foul
stench of decay all around me. I didn't
think of all the kids who had it so much
better than I did. No, I only saw the glow
of the street light, my salvation.

In way at this very moment, thousands
of miles away, and seemingly countless
years away now, is much like those moments
when I was a child. Once again I am trying
to escape. I realize now unlike then, that
I was only attempting to escape myself, the
life that I was born into. The saddest
reality one will ever know is when you
realize some seemingly stupid song lyrics
are so true that they are intrinsic to your
very soul. In my case it is the lyrics from

a Social Distortion song, "you can run all
of your life, and never go anywhere". I
guess in the end we always end up going
full circle, be that a good or bad thing is
up to your own perception.

Chap 1.

     As I sit in the bedroom of my
supposedly modern apartment looking out at
the street light I am lost, yet found.
Oddly all I can think of is the Buddhist
Four Noble Truths, or my version of them
anyway. First, all people will suffer, it
doesn't matter if you are a king or a hobo,

we all suffer in our own way. Second, it is one's own desires which will deliver us to our suffering. The bad part is that all I can think of is, damn do I have some fucked up desires. Shit it was just the other night that I fisted a woman's ass, and as fucked up as it is, I had always desired to do so. Third, you must be able to identify these fucked up desires that are forcing you to suffer, so as to fix the situation. Shit, I know my desires, I know they led me to my own suffering, but I still desire them, fucked up or not. Lastly, as I take it if you run down the list you can fix your situation, get rid of the desires and actions that led you to suffering. Well

this is always easier said than done. Yet
if you are able to do so, the premise is
that you will be happy, or at least
content.

Now all of this actually does make
sense if you really think about it. The
hard part was that it is so fucking simple
few would ever understand it. We humans
like to over analyze everything, nothing
can be simple. I am guilty as charged of
course, thus why at my age now I am still
fucked up, or as I was once called by a
woman, a man boy. I know it is time to deal
with it all, time to figure some shit out
if you will. I am no idiot, I know what the
causes of all of my suffering are. The

hardest part of it all is simply admitting
them out loud.

Fine then I will say it, the cause of
all of my suffering is females, women, and
bitches, whatever you want to call them.
Now we all know that the cause of all my
problems could never be me. Some deep
seeded psychosis like I resent my mom or
some shit. That she may have given me a
skewed version of how females are supposed
to be. No, all of my problems have to be
females and females alone, not me by any
means. Now you are laughing, you are
saying,

"No buddy you are fucked up and blaming
women, you are saying the same shit all men
do buddy". Well with this I would say that
you may just be wrong, let me have my
moment, it's one hundred percent the fault
of bitches okay. You see believe it or not
I was cursed before birth if you will. My
father passed his curse down upon me that
had been passed down upon him by his
father. Just how far back this curse goes
is anyone guess. I just accept the fact
that my blood has been cursed for all time.

It is this very curse that has led me
to believe many things most find disturbing
at best. For example, the idea of free will
is an utter illusion. All of you who

believe that you have actually chosen the paths in which you have traveled are simple minded fools. Come on people, do you really think that if there were a god, whatever the fuck you believe in, this god would actually allow you to bumble your way through your so called life? Please, don't be an idiot, if you are reading this I am already expecting that you are at least semi intelligent, well I hope so anyway. No my friends if you want to see how the idea of free will can and will be totally blown out of the water you need ask only a few questions my friends. Ask yourself, how many millions of coincidences had to take place for your grandparents to meet and for your parents to be born? Now ask yourself how many millions of these same coincidences had to take place for your parents to meet and you to be born? Now think of these same coincidences and allow that to be relative to all things. Now ask yourself how many trillions of coincidences took place from the big bang on? We all know that mathematics are the keys to the universe and I am sorry but the math does not add up. Don't be bummed out, just realize that you are either on a great journey with purpose designed by the gods, that or you are a mere pawn of their chess board, could go either way.

Back to the point, like my father before me I have allowed females to penetrate my life. Oh where to start, where to start right? I say that we start with the now and work our way backwards, seems to make sense. Does that sound good to you? It sounds good to me and I am the one writing this pile of crap so I guess it is how it will be then. I know, I know, on with it fucker I am already sick of this book and I can put it down at any moment. "LOL"

Chap 2.

I had long ago lost count of just how many females that I have actually slept with. All of their names are but mere memories that crossed my lips at one point if only for a mere moment in time. I loved them all for a moment. Yes that is my story and I am sticking to it, who are you to say that I didn't?

Oh the game, what is life but a simple game of chance, a roll of the dice? Oh the game, the game is far more than a simple game, no it is an art form. I have no clue as to where I learned the game, I was just born with the knowledge I guess. It is fucked up now and again, the things that simply come second nature to some of us.

Looking back on my life now I see that this once thought of gift that came second nature to me was actually a part of the curse cast down upon me. On the real, often I have envied those poor fools who don't have the ability, know how, just to scared, or what have you to play the game. I wish that I could be scared, I wish that I felt remorse.

The game or the art of working females is actually very simple. Like a game you see all females and their sexual pleasures as your opponents. The point is to get into their minds, to light the spark that makes them unable to let you go. Pussy is what you would think would be the end goal, but you would be wrong. Pussy is nice, very nice, yet I am sorry it is not the end goal of the game. Well it could be the aim of some, but it is not for me. You see I want them to love me, if only for a single moment in time. Pussy, shit any man can get pussy from any girl if he works hard enough. Shit even a lame fuck can get pussy, if he don't have the right words he can always use booze or drugs, they are just lames. No, pussy is simple, getting a woman to desire you, to love you, to need you, now that takes talent.

Now I know this sounds fucked up right, who knows maybe it is? I guess that no matter how you actually look at it I am a fucked up person. You see the more perfect that something is, the less likely that I will be to except it. You see this too is part of the curse, part of my destiny I suppose? Remember what I told you earlier, I do not believe in free will. No, everything that happens is all a part of a play. This play is being put on for the mere enjoyment of the gods. One would hope that this is all to learn a lesson of some sort. That once they learn what we need we can move on to the next level of spiritually, but this is just a hope.

I have never once understood what the fuck a woman would possibly see in me? I have never considered myself even remotely good looking, even when I was a kid. I have always thought that I have an odd look at best, a bit awkward to be honest if you will. I am not a particularly tall guy, I am not short either, just over six foot. As well I am no small man, I'd actually say that I am a bit fat really. Now these would all be deterrents as I would see it for any female.

No, it's all about my personality. I like to think that I am a fun guy over all. I am smart as well, to smart actually for my own good. I have been told that I am border line arrogant, and possibly a bit of an asshole, but I don't see myself that way. Those people who say that are just jealous. Yet this so called perceived arrogance should also work as a deterrent to thwart any sort of sexual liaisons with them. Well one would think this anyway, yet it is seldom the case. Oddly, most females tend to see this very attribute I would expect them to hate as a turn on, stupid bitches.

I do feel that it is the life style that I have chosen, or was chosen for me that allows me ample booty. I have to admit I have never been like everyone else, rather I have always been just on the edge of normal society. My whole life I have been a musician, an artist, a writer, a tattoo artist, a body piercer, and a painter. I never chose these paths, I would have rather been a banker, no they chose me. I will tell you that I have never done any of these things in an attempt to get laid. Rather it has been just the opposite, to be honest I expected my lifestyle choices would drive females far away from me. The banker, well the banker has security, and in the end they marry him, they just want to fuck me. I am fucked really, no matter what I do, how well I think that I am doing it. I can't stop creating, just another part of the curse. I can't stop writing, I can't stop painting, and I can't stop playing music. I am compelled to just keep going on and on

putting words on paper, paint on canvas,
and musical notes in the air, I am fucked.
Music, oh music, music has always been a
passion of mine all of my life. Be it at
home or on a stage I must play. As of late
I can't stop painting, an empty canvas, an
empty wall, I have to fill it with art.

You see I am a flake, the banker is
steady and true, me I am fucked, there is
nothing stable about me, any artist for
that matter. Yet females are drawn to us
like flies to shit, and many of us are just
that, shit. Despite our many quirks it is
those very quirks that drive females to us,
and of course me. I am a bucket list fuck!
Women all want the artist, musician, or

writer just once. They all know that it will never last, they just want the experience. They are attracted to what sets us apart, that idea that we see something other men never will, and we do. Females are not stupid for the most part, the reality of just how fucked up we are kicks in very soon, no matter how much they thought that they could change us. After a relationship with me, a woman looks at that banker more and more, despite the fact they know they will be bored. I guess bored is better than heart-broken? I am an object relegated to their past. Something they can reminisce with their girlfriends about. I may have been the most exciting, the best sex she ever had, perfect yet so flawed in so many ways, in the end security always wins out. I don't blame them, it is what it is.

Chap 3.

I am at work, I meet a girl. She is a cute little brunette, sexy little white girl. I crack a few jokes, shoot her a smile, and drop her a business card. I tell her that she can drop me a text at any time. I never once ask her number, this is all by design of course. I don't have to flirt with her at all, I just can't help myself. Shit, I know four girls right now who would be pissed if I said that I didn't have a girlfriend. Hell that cute little white girl has a husband, yet not even an hour after giving her my card she is texting me. Innocent text at first, then as they progress they get dirtier and dirtier. Soon she is damn near sucking me off through text. I have done nothing, yet she is already asking if she can come see me when I get off work, I am weak, yet all powerful so of course I say yes.

Reality is that I am texting four other girls at the same time that I am texting her, always hedging my bets. One of

my supposed girlfriends comes up to my
work, we go in my room and shut the door.
She drops to her knee's she looks so good
on her knee's sucking my cock. I so love
the way she works her mouth up and down.

I love light skin girls with dark hair
and blue eyes. She looks up at me with
those big blue eyes and my cock in her
hands, I love you daddy, she says. I love
you to baby, I lie. This false statement
just makes her suck me that more intensely,
she knows it's a lie, but it is what she
wants to hear. As I hold the back of her
head I can feel myself welling up from
within. My knees begin to shake a bit, I
let go. With a rush of energy I fill my

sweet princess's mouth with the keys to my soul, which she readily swallows down.

I pretend to talk to her for the next half an hour, as if I don't want her to just leave. Thank the gods I start to get busy and my little princess makes her way off for home. She isn't gone five minuet's and I am talking to the girl I met earlier. Some may see this as fucked up, for me it is just life.

After a few hours my day is done and I am heading home. My new toy I met earlier is damn near begging to come over to my place. I actually call her and give her my address, no traceable evidence. Once home I

hit the shower to wash off my previous
sins. I go around my place and light a few
candles and spray some air freshener.
Within a half an hour she is at my door.
This is all her idea but I can tell that
she is a bit on edge so I get her a glass
of wine. I give her a little tour of my
place, she is in awe. I show her my many
paintings I have done and am working on.
Personally I think my art sucks sometimes,
even so she is in love with it. She is
looking at my guitars all around the house.
In a way I feel exposed, she is fascinated,
yet in a way I am out there naked, she is
in my head if you will. Yet we are both
playing a game, she came here to get

fucked, I invited her so I could get fucked. Right now we are doing the dance.

We are talking on the couch, I slip in a quick kiss the kiss turns to heavy petting. Before I know it she has her shirt and bra off. I am playing with and sucking on her nice fake breast. I am surprised by them, I have seen so many and I have to admit the doctor did a great job. It is only a matter of moments and she is on her knees sucking my dick. She is good damn good, her husband trained her well. I have found far too often that when you mess with these married girls they turn out to be like that never been kissed flick. I look down at her as she is blowing me, she looks up at me with big beautiful brown eyes. Despite how beautiful her eyes are I can't take my eyes off the huge fucking rock on her finger. That damn ring has to be at least five carrots. Shit that didn't even count all of the small diamonds on the ring behind it. I laugh to myself, someone must really love this girl. That or it is just far cheaper to keep her.

We move to the bed and instantly she jumps on top of me. I like the way that she rides me, I have been with hundreds of women and she honestly stands out, good job baby girl I think. She grinds down hard on my cock, taking every bit of cock deep inside of her. In a weird way I have always hated when a women does that, it can go wrong and be painful real quick.

I enjoy watching her ride me, she is just so into it. I lean forward and grab her throat and squeeze just a little bit, just enough to slightly cut off her breath. She moans even louder, so I pull her hair back now and grasp her just a little bit harder. She lets go and begins to cum, fucking my sheets all up.

I get on top of her and begin to pound her into my bed. I then grab her and flip her over on her side and begin to hit it from the side. As I push my cock inside of her I pull back on her hair and ask her if she is my good girl or my dirty whore? Once again she starts to cum as she calls out I'm your whore daddy. I pound her tight pussy, ass in the air for the next fifteen minutes. My new pet keeps coming over and over again, I must be doing something right. She is so wet each time I push into her I feel her juices covering me, the sex sounds like a wet boot in the mud. I push her down on her stomach and push my cock up her ass. She moans with joy, dirty little whore. I grab the back of her head and push her face into the pillow as I pound her from behind. I am letting her know that I am the man, I am in charge of this new relationship, and she can't quit Cumming. I let go and fill her ass full of my essence.

I stand up and walk to the bathroom and wash my dick off. She quickly gets up and attempts to straighten herself up a bit. Once again I find myself trying to talk to a woman wanting nothing more than for her to leave. She looks at her phone, holy shit look at the time, I have to go my husband will be home soon, she says. I walk her to the door and give her a kiss. She walks down to her car and disappears into the night. I sit down in my big man chair take out my phone and enter her name under married bitch. I have no clue what her actual name is, to be honest I can care less. The odds are I will never see this girl again unless she gets horny and needs a booty call. Shit I probably saved her marriage, now she will bang her old man and think of me, I did a good thing tonight. You see can be a good dude.

Chap 4.

That night I slept as calm and as soundly as the dead. You want to know a fucked a reality, I don't even remember that bitches name, that's on the real. I am left to wonder if anyone actually has a name. I know mine, it was given to me, yet

I rarely go by it, so does it really matter, the name given you that is? I don't know, most people see this process of thought as that of a man who is cold and uncaring. Personally, I know that I should care, I know that I should feel like a piece of shit for fucking every woman who walks. Well, I am sorry but no matter how much I do try, well I just don't. I whole heartily do not give a single shit, in fact I care so little that the mere idea of caring seldom crosses my mind. I often wonder if maybe this is a flaw in my genetic makeup, or possibly I never evolved. Yeah that's it, I am a genetic relic from a gone by era, the era of the pack leader.

No, this day and age despite what people say is one of conservatism and fear. Well, let me rephrase that, it all depends on where you live. Me, I live in Las Vegas Nevada, it is easy to say that you can be whatever the hell you want here. Yet this is still America and America is a land of religious oppression. Most Americans have been taught that every impulse that they have is wrong or even evil. Religion has taught people that simply being human is a crime that should be punished. Religion has taught us that we are so much higher and mightier than all of the mammals on this planet we all share. Personally I don't share this view, we are all animals, just afraid to admit it.

I hate this concept I truly do, this idea people have that they are so high and mighty on the food chain. I take the Satanist view here, I always have and always will. I do not feel that I am any better than any animal, in fact I am, probably worse. No I have no visions of grandeur, I just have a nicer cave than most other beast. Maybe it is thought processes such as these that make me so fucked up? By thinking that we are no better than the beast that walk this earth,

I guess I put everyone in this animal grouping, makes sense to me any way.

I wake up, it's nine AM. I am a man of this modern age thus the first thing that I look at is my phone. Sadly, and I hate to admit this but my phone is the last thing I look at as well. Hum, I have a text from a girl named Katie. She works at noon and wants to have a bit of fun before she goes to work. I am weak, of course I hit her back and tell her to come over. She tells me that she is already on her way so I hop in a quick shower.

There is nothing better than a hot shower in the morning. The hot water pours over my body, I can feel each and every

pore open up from the heat. The soap enters

each and every pore cleansing the sins from

my body. I am always shocked by the amount

of dirt and oils our pores collect in a

day, it's kind of gross really. I am

brushing my teeth, a hot shower and brushed

teeth allow us, or me anyway to feel human.

I remember once not being able to shower

for several days, man did I feel gross.

I have barely dried off and put my gym

shorts on when Katie is knocking on the

door. Katie walks in like she owns the

place, or me anyway. She waste no time as

always, she knows what she wants and

exactly how to get it. It isn't two minutes

and all of her clothes are on the floor.
She grabs me and begins kissing me like a
drunken stripper. Katie is a bit fucked in
the head, she likes her sex ruff, I mean
real ruff. I decide to just go with it,
give her what she so desires. I grab Katie
by the throat, pull her hair back and bite
down into the side of her neck. Secretly I
have always wanted to be a vampire, yet I
don't know if I could give up the sunlight.
Katie moans out loud like some sort of
horny beast. I look into her face and call
her a whore as I push her down onto her
knees. Katie takes my cock into her mouth
and begins slamming it down her own throat,
attempting to gag herself with it. Katie

takes it all of the way down and licks my balls at the same time. When she decides that she needs a breath Katie pulls back, covering the two of us in her drool. I love the way it feels when this girl sucks cock, this bitch craves it. I can't help but wonder how many cocks this whore had to suck to get so good? Yet hey, who the fuck am I to judge my past is fucking terrible. Who is really the fucking whore?

I pull Katie off of my cock by her long blonde hair and slap her in the face pretty damn hard, it has to be hard for her to get off. Katie is kinky, but so am I. I go to my night stand and pull out some hand cuffs, a blind fold, and a cat of nine tails. Katie is blind folded and cuffed to the bed, time to play, pleasure and pain, a fine line at best. I bury my face in between her legs, I love eating pussy, shit I am a fucking pro to be real with you. I love eating this little slut's pussy in particular, it just looks so damn perfect. I challenge any man, hell even women to look at this perfect soft pink pussy and not want to devour it. I have seen countless pussies and Katie's is seriously one of the top five prettiest pussies I have ever seen.

Not only does Katie's pussy look perfect but it taste so, so, sweet. I am left to wonder if god himself didn't design

every aspect of this girl's pussy. To top
it off and maybe why it taste so good and
looks so good is the fact that she is in
perfect health. Katie is a vegan, as well
as a yoga girl. She only eats healthy and
lives healthy, well other than her sexual
taste. For all of you girls reading,
remember eat healthy and you will get that
pussy eaten, works the same for us guys, we
are what we eat.

Katie has already cum at least five
times when I roll her over. This is why
girls love fucking me, I am not greedy, I
let them get theirs. I don't fuck Katie yet
though, she is still tied up and blind
folded. I take my cat of nine tails and

whip her across her ass rather hard. Katie moans with joy as I whip her over and over again, I have no clue why she enjoys this, but like I said, I don't judge we all have our kinks. After whipping her making her cum again and again I get behind her and push my cock into her dripping wet pussy. I twist and contort Katie into every position possible, all while she is still blind folded and cuffed to the bed. It is sexy to watch her contort into so many fucked up positions. Finally I can't take much more I pull out of her and shove my cock down her throat as I finger her ass and pussy. I let her fuck my hand, two fingers in her ass two fingers in her pussy. I move to her pussy and work my whole fist inside of her, Katie begins to squirt everywhere. I grab my belt and loop it around Katie's neck and get behind her, her ass up doggy style. I push my cock up her ass and begin to pound her like the whore she is, no mercy. Pulling back on her throat with my belt I pull out and force her face in front of me. I let go and cover Katie's face with my demon seed. I let her drop back onto the bed as I do the same. My bed is fucked, it may as well be a swimming pool. I look over at Katie she has pulled her blind fold off, looking at me, cum all over her face, fucking whore, fucking beautiful whore.

Chap 5.

I don't think that Katie stays longer than fifteen twenty minuet's after we are done fucking. To be honest with you I don't know if I used her or she used me, does it really matter? The reality is that other than sex I can't stand that fucking girl. As far as I am concerned Katie is just some stupid ass whore, a simple piece of pussy, be it a good one or not. The bitch uses me as I use women, she wants a good dicking and some abuse, and I'm good for both. Not many women will let you do the shit she wants me to do to her mouth, I won't really even get into what she wants done to her ass. Katie has some rich old dude that takes care of her for the most part. She has a nice ass house that he pays for, she drives a nice as little M class BMW, and she has a decent amount of cash in her bank account. She only works because she likes to get out of the house. Makes me wish I was a chick sometime shit, all she has to do is give up some random pussy and her life is charmed. I don't think he can or will do what I do though, I mean the depraved shit. You know, now I think of it she has never let me even go to her house.

I ask myself who is worse, Katie or me, I think that we are both fucked to be honest. While Katie likes to be abused, I enjoy doing it. Who is more fucked up then,

I honestly enjoy hurting her that is twisted in itself. I get a thrill wrapping a belt around her throat and choking her to the point of her passing out. I enjoy whipping her to till her body is red from the lashes. I enjoy slapping the shit out of her as if she were not even human at all.

Katie enjoys all of this, hell she loves all of this. Is that fucked up at all? Is it fucked up that she revels in pain and humiliation, or that I revel in dispensing this pain and humiliation? I don't know nor do I care, it's a fucking blast. If she is fucked so be it, if I am fucked so be it. Like I said earlier everything comes down to perspective.

Chap 6.

After taking a nice hot shower I once again get a text, it's from Elizabeth. I like Elizabeth, she is older than I am, I think she told me forty three, but who knows she could be telling me a lie. I have seldom found it smart to trust a woman in any real way, even less so if it has anything what so ever to do with their age. Either way, or despite her age whatever it may be, Elizabeth is beautiful. She spends a lot of time in the gym and eats super healthy. This coupled with a juicy ass and

some perfectly sculpted size D breast makes
her look perfect to the eye.

Now one would think that I would be all
fucked out by now. I will say that for most
men this assumption would be very correct
to ascertain. Yet with me there is never
really fucked out. You see I have realized
something, I am a sex addict, yes, and I am
addicted to sex. I get ten times more booty
than even a well fed man if you will. Yet,
despite this I am never satisfied, I always
want more, like a fat kid at a buffet
filled with sweets. You have no clue how
many times that I have wished I could just
be satisfied, just be normal, it just don't
work for me, the curse remember? Don't get

it twisted this reality that I live with is fucked up, but we can get to that later.

Elizabeth tells me that she is in the neighborhood and wants to stop by. Of course I tell her that she can, the reality is that I am excited and happy to see her. I have to admit I actually enjoy Elizabeth's company, and you have no clue how rare that is for me. I quickly spray air freshener all over the apartment. I coat the bed and bedroom with as much as I can and not make it noxious. It is always best to get the scent of sex from the room as much as possible before the next woman arrives. I go all out with Elizabeth, I light a fifteen dollar Yankee Candle, and bitches always love the smell of Yankee Candles. Men, the mere fact that you even have them in your home will turn a woman on. I next focus on myself, fresh deodorant and of course my best designer imposter cologne. That's right I am far too cheap to buy the real shit, so what?

Now so fresh and so clean, clean I hear a knock at the door. Instantly I think of the Raven, I love Poe, a gentle rapping on my chamber door. I open the door and see my sexy older lady, soccer mom, milf, beautiful Elizabeth. Is she really older though? I am getting older now, older than I ever thought that I would to be honest. Elizabeth is a doctor, yeah how the fuck did I score classy pussy like that you are asking yourself, well I ask myself the same thing. She is always dressed so, so nice. I just look at my sweet queen for a moment, her nice skirt, her reserved yet sexy blouse, and of course her eight hundred dollar pumps. I so love a woman in heels, classy. Elizabeth is always decked out in her jewelry as well. When I look at her there is nothing that I can find that isn't just pure sexy, she is beautiful.

My sweet doctor is more old school than Katie, she actually attempts to have a conversation with me. I enjoy this greatly, most of my women are just fucking whores that all want to go straight to fucking. I tell Elizabeth about work and other random shit, leaving a lot out of course. She tells me all about the hospital and its politics, all the crazy shit that goes on there. She then tells me about some dude that she is seeing who lives in Frisco. I guess that he is a surgeon and comes down every two weeks to see her. Elizabeth marvels at a new painting that I had just finished, saying how much that she wanted it for her office or study.

While I enjoy her company I am sick of talking, I lean and begin kissing my queen. I kiss her on the neck, this always drives her wild, all bitches classy or not love having their necks kissed and nibbled on. I unbutton and drop Elizabeth's blouse onto the floor, unhooking her bra in the process. I love looking at that ten thousand dollar boob job, as I handle her breast as only a man can. I assure you guys there is a difference between handling a woman's breast and man handling them. I work my way down Elizabeth's chest and stomach till I drop her skirt off and lay her on the bed exposing her sexy G string. I work my way up her thighs, kissing and licking paying attention to every inch. This is a real woman, there is no rush job here. Any fool can just jump in the pussy, I call these idiots unseasoned. If you are like me and attempt what I am doing you will have any woman Cumming before your tongue even hits her pussy, I'm a pro. Finally after working my way to Elizabeth's pussy I can see that she is already dripping wet, it is now and only now that I bury my face into her wanting pussy. As I work my tongue I work two fingers into her pussy arced up of course to work her G spot, yes guys it does exist.

Dr. Liz is working her hips now, riding my face. As she is fucking my face I can feel her entire body shuttering, she lets go over and over again covering my face with her juices. Of course I don't stop, no this drives me more I keep going only now with a fury. I go until Elizabeth can take no more, her body simply can't take it. I told you, I love eating pussy, I take this serious. Shit, I need to take something serious in life right?

Elizabeth gets on top of me and begins to ride me. I love to just look up at this vision of beauty as she rides me. Just watching her cum over and over again lets me know that fucking is my true calling. Anyway, she loves riding my cock, I would be an asshole not to let her. Shit, Elizabeth does so much good for so many people I feel it is my duty to give to her, and my gift to her is orgasm after orgasm. The only thing I do to her not of the norm is lightly slap her calling her my dirty

little girl, shit likes that nothing
extreme at all. Few females deserve my
respect, even fewer get it, but Elizabeth
not only deserves it but receives it as
well.

As is the case with Elizabeth I let
her ride me until she can no longer move.
It's nice, when she gets off of me it
sounds like a wet boot being pulled from
the mud, the sound of good sex. I lay her
on her back and spread her legs as far as
they can go before I push my sin inside of
her. Here I take no mercy on my sweet
doctor, no rather I beat her pussy like it
owes me money. My nice reserved doctor is
now screaming like a little whore. I love

hearing her scream out fuck me daddy as I pound her into the bed. I feel like these are words that should never cross her lips, its dirty yet elegant. Yet this makes me sad as well, her screaming out like a whore only serves to remind me that my queen is just like the others, just like the rest of them, a fucking whore.

Now I see her as a whore, I roll my queen over, her juicy ass up in the air doggy style. I see her different all of a sudden I begin to pound her pussy as if she were a Tijuana hooker that I had just paid a mere twenty dollars to. I pull my cock from her dripping wet pussy and spit onto my hand. She is already so wet this isn't really needed, more symbolic if anything. I rub my spit down my already dripping cock and push it up my queen's ass. Reserved or not Elizabeth is a fucking whore and all whores enjoy being pounded in their asses. I am far from gentle now as I pound her ass. I want this whore to leave knowing that she had been fucked hours after she had gone. Elizabeth pounds back onto my cock as I thrust forward till I can't take it anymore. I feel my body well up, I release filling my queen's ass full of my sin.

Elizabeth turns around taking my cock into her mouth. This fucking whore wants every last drop of my sin, as if by taking it within her she will gain my power. She sucks me to the point in which I can't take anymore. As I lay on my bed Elizabeth gets up and begins to straighten herself up and get dressed. It is sexy to just lay there and watch her. She tells me that she wants my new painting for her office. I tell her that she can have it, I'd give her anything really. Of course she insist on paying and won't let up. I give in and tell her leave whatever she feels that it is worth on the table before she leaves. I get up and give her a kiss and tell her I am hopping in the shower. Elizabeth tells me she will let herself out and kisses me, thanking me for the great time, I feel like the woman sometimes with this bitch.

After a nice shower I walk out into the living room. Secretly I hoped that Elizabeth would still be there, but of course she has gone. Elizabeth has taken my painting. I looked over on the table and saw ten one hundred dollar bills. Fuck it, I need the money but she could have taken the painting for free. I hold the money in my hand, wow a thousand bucks, does this make me a hooker?

Chap 7.

It isn't even an hour and I am thinking of texting yet another girl. I know that this is fucked up, yet I told you I don't know what is wrong with me. I told you that I feel like some huge fat guy at a buffet, as far as I can see I see food, only my food is pussy. Yet like that fat guy no matter how much food I eat I am never satisfied, full or not I can't help but go back for more. Shit even if I was full I would follow the path of the Romans and go to the vomitorium and puke so I could keep going, it's a sickness. I know and how do I know that there is something very wrong with me.

     I wasn't always like this, no there

was a time that I was a one woman type of

guy. Shit that seems like another life time

ago though. Maybe it was, maybe I am

reliving the same shit, all a part of my

curse. I was a young kid when I met her,

just barely out of my teens. I say I was a

kid because I know now that I was not yet a

man. Her name, well her name really matters

not at this point, let's just say that her

name wasn't bitch or whore. I had no clue

as to how or why, but I knew that she and I

would meet, I just knew. I guess it was one

of those odd gifts from the gods, that or a

foreshadowing of my fucked off future. I

told you before that the gods use us as

pawns in their personal games of chess. I

know now that meeting her was a fucked off

joke played upon me by the gods. They

wanted to torture me, they wanted to play

their fucked up games with my very soul.

Either way, when I very first saw her I

knew that she was the one, long before I

ever learned her name.

I first saw her in an elevator while I

was standing with my current girlfriend. I

tried my hardest not to look at her to very

hard, yet I know that anyone who saw me

knew that I was attracted to her. I can't

lie I couldn't look away from her at all, I

had seen her in my dreams. I know that

sounds fucked up but I am telling you the

one hundred percent truth. I played it off with my girlfriend at the time saying how she looked familiar, yet I just couldn't place her. I even went as far as to ask if we had ever come across her at a party before. My girlfriends own arrogance didn't allow her to see that I was head over heels in love with the girl from the elevator.

I couldn't get her face out of my mind. When I made love to my girlfriend it was only to the girl from the elevator. All I could do was think of my mystery girl from the elevator with her army jacket with its little German flag. She had long dark hair, not just dark it was pretty much black. I could tell that her hair was super thick, I knew that if only I could touch it that it was certain to feel like silk. Her skin was dark, so beautifully dark, yet not black girl dark. I had always liked dark skin girls, just a turn on to me. She was a rather short girl, at least compared to all the girls that I knew anyway. I didn't think that she was much taller than five foot that may be giving her an inch or two even. She was not some tiny little skinny girl either, which had always been what I went for. No my dream girl from the elevator was actually on the semi thick side. She was nothing like my current girlfriend at the time who was a near six foot blonde. This didn't mean shit to me though, all I wanted was my girl from the elevator.

The gods play their games and oh how do they play them well. Some would say that it was a coincidence, some would just say simple chance, and others would say it was just plain dumb luck. I knew then as I do now that there is no chance, it was all a part of my destiny. Before I had ever told anyone of my dream girl I had been told by a fortune teller who told me of the exact girl from my dreams. It was odd this fortune teller told me exactly what I already knew. Now I am not making this up, this was an experience I had clear back in high school, long before my dream girl and I had ever met.

No, what happened next only helped to prove two things to me. First, there is no such thing as coincidence. Secondly, that the mere idea of free will did not exist. No despite all aspects of chance this dream woman of mine walked right into my very house during a party. It was when I saw her in my home that everything came clear to me, everything made sense. How many random so called acts of chance had to take place for this moment to happen I couldn't help but think? Shit the number was countless, fucking countless, unfathomable to be real with you. From her parents meeting and

having her, to mine meeting and having me.
Hell, as far as I am concerned these so
called random acts of chance could be
traced all the way back to Adam and Eve.
For her to haunt my dreams for years, this
just couldn't be, her here in my living
room. No the simple act of her being here
proved to me right then and there that the
gods love placing us all on a stage, simply
performing a play for their mere enjoyment,
fucking assholes.

Chap 8.

We were drawn to one another like
moths to a flame. Destiny, oh destiny is

one of those things that two people can never deny or attempt to fight. No this path had already been put into place long before either one of us were ever born. Even if we wanted to fight the destiny lain out before us the gods would never have allowed it. This is the way of the gods, we are all at the will of the universe, and believe me you the universe never makes mistakes. With the blessing or the mere will of the gods we fell deeply in love. Hell, does the sun know when it's glowing, does the grass know when it's growing?

Time flies when you are happy, in fact time itself seems to cease to exist at all. Within the blink of an eye years had passed, yet I would have struggled to tell you just how many and when. There was no other woman for me, hell no one compared to my queen, none but her worth a second glance. This is what I would call the blessed time in my life. I had the woman of my dreams, literally the fucking woman from my dreams. I also had the one thing that I had never known before, a working relationship and stability. I had never known anyone with a working relationship in all of my life, be it friends or their parents. All I had ever known was dysfunction, and to be honest I had no clue what stability even was. Here I was a married man, a dream of mine since I was a kid. I had everything that I had ever wanted, or thought that I wanted anyway, the woman of my dreams, a home, a great job, a life, hell I even had a little dog and a cat.

Well we all know where this is going now don't we? You already know that I am obviously not with this dream girl now, that this is that part in the beginning we had talked about earlier, well you are right. Oh how the gods love to play with their toys, now and again like a child a bit to ruff if you will. Looking back I feel that I was a simple player in a Greek tragedy. It seemed that each way that I turned the gods purposely spun me in the

opposite direction. All the while I saw
them laughing at my turmoil, but hey that
is life right?

No the gods allowed me to know love,
to know what I perceived as happiness, to
know what these things actually felt like.
You see, you can't miss something that you
have never known. It was this simple fact
that the gods waited until I thought my
life was perfect to take everything away
from me. All of the comfort that I had
known was ripped from me, my entire world
thrown upside down. Yet, this was all
seemingly done for me in slow motion, or at
least replayed for me in such a manner. All
that I had taken for granted was now gone.

The intense love that I had known was now resentment and anger. All the happy times I had known were filled with anger and fighting, that I could not possibly figure out just how it had begun. I wish that I could tell you where it all started to go wrong, but to be honest I have no real clue.

It wasn't long before I found myself kicked out of the home that I had helped to build. I was left to wonder if I had made a deal with the Devil in a past life and he had come to collect his due. Oh the Devil, what a crafty fucker he is. You see the Devil is a real fucking prick, yet a

fucking genius at the same time, remember
made in gods image.

A man ask the Devil to know happiness,
to know love. Of course the Devil says no
problem buddy sign here, and like a fool
you do so. Then the Devil makes good on his
end of the bargain. The Devil never lies,
no the Devil just omits parts of the story.
The next thing you know is that you are
happier than you have ever been in all your
life.

In fact, you are happier than you had
ever even dreamed of, happier than you
could have ever even imagined. Then in the
Devils true fashion, just when you are

truly content, truly happy, the Devil steps back into your life. You see you asked the Devil to know happiness, you asked the Devil to know love, you never asked for these gifts to last for your whole life. Now this is your bad, you didn't read the fine print, the Devil got you in the technicalities. This is where he got me, fucking technicalities.

Once you have had something and you have had it all taken away from you, well let's just say it sucks at a whole different level. I know now this was all just a part of my destiny, the cards dealt to me many life time's ago. Don't get shit twisted, all of your decisions are planned

out, everything leads you to your destiny.
The gods deal you a hand from a stacked
deck, all you can do is just deal with it,
it just is what it is.

They say that it is better to have
loved and lost than to have never loved at
all. Now this is where I call bullshit,
total utter fucking bullshit. Love is like
doing coke, or like how you feel after you
get your first piece of ass, you can never
have enough. After you have had whatever it
is that sets you off you will always chase
it till the end of your days. You end up a
slave to it, sometimes losing just who it
is that you even are during the process.
You end up like Bruce Willis in the Sixth

Sense movie if you will, despite all the signs you don't even know that you are dead.

For many, many years I have wandered if you will, a lost soul. Then one day it all hit me like a bullet in the head, just why I slept with every fucking woman that walked. I didn't do it because of some bullshit idea of the game. I didn't have sex with all of these girls because I was some super stud. I didn't play with all of these poor girl's hearts and souls because I was some cold hearted fuck. No, I am Bruce Willis when the kid told him that he saw dead people and often they didn't even know that they were dead. All of the signs began to fit if you will, which I must

admit is rather depressing to be honest. I

have done and do the things that I do for

one reason and one reason only. I am

looking to find but a single glimpse of the

happiness that I once had.

It is this very glimpse that I was

allowed to see that ensures the fact that I

will never see it again. Yet like a crack

head chasing his or her first hit, I go on

and on in vain, searching like a fool. Each

day and night I look for love between

countless girls thighs, knowing that I will

never find that for which I quest. I know

that I am forsaken, that I am like a ghost

doomed to forever roam the earth for all

eternity.

In the end I am an imposter, I am not

what you think that I am. I am not some mac

daddy pimp, I am not some big player, and I

am surely not some super stud. No these are

things fools see from the outside looking

in at my life. The truth is that I am a

lost man, looking for something he will

never have again. Worse of all I know

exactly what I am looking for, how it

feels, how it taste, it is a lost dream.

Each and every girl that I fuck day in and

day out only helps to heighten my

suffering. With each one of them a piece of

me dies inside, knowing that they have only

shown me pain and heartache. I know what I am doing is wrong, I know I won't find what I am looking for, I know I should just stop before I hurt someone else. I am unsure if I am still looking for love, all I lost, or if I am just punishing myself for losing it on purpose. Maybe I am punishing all of these women for the crime of simply not being her.

So, here I sit all alone in my dark and lonely room. I am the same guy that you met in the beginning of this tale I assure you, only now I hope that you just see me in a different light. I am that guy who is all alone in the end, that guy who has no one to tell him that they love him and truly mean it. I am that guy in his bed in his dark room looking out at the street light once again, the same thing I have done since I was a child. Sitting, looking at the glow of the street light, lost in its sheen, wishing that I could escape myself.